TIME TRAIN TO THE BLITZ

SOPHIE McKENZIE

USBORNE

CONTENTS

For Cliona

First published in the UK in 2010 by Usborne Publishing Ltd., Usborne House, 83-85 Saffron Hill, London EC1N 8RT, England. www.usborne.com

Cover illustration by Scott Altmann.
Black and white illustrations by Ian McNee.

A CIP catalogue record for this book is available from the British Library.

JF AMJJASOND/10 95837 ISBN 9780746097533
Printed in Reading, Berkshire, UK.

1 PIPPY DISAPPEARS

The day the Time Train found them was much like any other. Joe and Scarlett were throwing a ball for their dog, Pippy, in the park near their new house.

Joe looked round, bored. The park was small and dull, with a children's playground at one end and a small wood at the other.

"Let me throw it," Scarlett whined.

"In a minute." Joe chucked a long, straight ball towards the trees.

Pippy scampered after it, picked it up between her teeth and brought it back to him. She was a small, brown Jack Russell with a white splodge of fur over one eye. Officially Pippy belonged to the whole family, but everyone knew she was really Joe's dog.

Joe petted Pippy where she liked it best – on the back of her head right between her two soft ears. His phone beeped. A text from Mum.

Tea ready. Come home. Love Mum x

Joe sighed. Ever since they'd moved this had been the pattern of the summer holidays. Get up, play in the park with Pippy and Scarlett, then home when Mum called.

Scarlett snatched up the ball. "My turn," she said triumphantly.

Joe shrugged. "We have to go home," he said.

"But I want a go." Scarlett chucked the ball high into the air. It sailed up...up...and right into the middle of the wood.

Pippy tore towards it and disappeared from sight. Joe stood, waiting, for a few seconds. But the dog didn't reappear.

"Here, Pippy," he called, scanning the trees for a glimpse of her brown and white fur.

There was no sign. Joe's heart thudded. Pippy *always* came when he called.

"Pippy!" he called, running towards the trees. "Come here!"

He stopped on the edge of the wood. The trees were large and leafy and set close together. It seemed darker and quieter now than when they'd ventured in before.

"Look, Joe." Scarlett raced up beside him. She pointed into the wood. "There's Pippy."

Joe squinted into the gloom. There was Pippy,

trotting between some trees, sniffing at the ground. Joe's shoulders relaxed with relief. "Here, girl," he shouted.

But Pippy ignored him.

"Pippy," Joe yelled, feeling a little annoyed. She *must* be able to hear him. Why didn't she come?

He darted into the wood. As he walked under the cover of the trees the air seemed to darken and hush.

"Pippy," he shouted again.

This time the dog looked up. But instead of running to Joe, she just wagged her tail. Like she wanted him to come over and play.

"Come on, Pippy," Joe insisted. "We have to go home."

But Pippy darted backwards, tail wagging. "Woof!" She sniffed at the ground again.

Joe looked down and frowned. Pippy was

sniffing at a line of peculiar tracks on the ground. Joe couldn't tell what they were made of, but they glowed with a weird fluorescent light.

Pippy wagged her tail and splayed her paws over the tracks.

"Come *on.*" Joe tried to grab her collar, but the dog skipped away.

Joe shook his head. Pippy had *never* disobeyed him before. What was she doing?

A bead of sweat trickled down Joe's neck. It was spooky here under the trees. The air was thick and heavy, giving Joe the sense that the world around him was waiting for something to happen. And those tracks Pippy was playing on were definitely well beyond weird. They were glowing more fiercely now, almost orange in the dim shadow of the trees.

A strange, thin *whee* sounded in the distance.

"What was that?" asked Scarlett.

11

"Sounded a bit like a train whistle," Joe said. "Maybe that's what those weird tracks are here for...a train."

"A train track?" Scarlett wrinkled her nose. "But we're in a park."

Joe reached for Pippy again and missed. "Come *on*!"

Pippy gambolled away, then stood, quite still, on the tracks. She cocked her ears. The ground trembled. Hairs stood up on the back of Joe's neck.

"Did you feel that?" Scarlett said.

Joe nodded. Pippy wagged her tail, as if nothing were wrong. "Come on, girl," he urged.

As he spoke the sky darkened again and the glow of the train tracks grew stronger.

"Joe, what's happening?" Scarlett cried.

The *whee* sound pierced through Joe's head

again. The sky was dark as night now. A bright light shone in the distance. Pippy barked. Joe's mouth was dry. The bright light was moving towards them. The ground rumbled. A loud roar filled the air.

"It's a train," Joe shouted. "It's coming."

He reached out for Pippy again. Grabbed her collar. Tugged.

The light surged closer and closer.

"Get Pippy!" Scarlett yelled. "Get her off those tracks!"

The light filled the air around them. Just three metres away.

"Pippy!" Joe yelled. She was digging her paws into the ground, refusing to move from the tracks. He pulled harder at her collar. "Pippy, *please*!"

Two metres. The train hurtled towards them.

"Joe, MOVE!" Scarlett screamed.

Pippy wasn't budging. And Joe couldn't leave her.

One metre.

Joe closed his eyes and waited for the crash.

2 THE TIME TRAIN

A gust of air whooshed past Joe's ears. He opened his eyes, his hand still gripping Pippy's collar. The train had stopped centimetres in front of them. The sky above them brightened.

"Wow," Scarlett breathed.

Joe blinked. The train standing in front of him now wasn't like any he'd seen before. It was the usual train shape – long, with a rounded front end, like a bottle-nosed dolphin. But it was made from the same glowing material as the train tracks, pulsing with a faint fluorescent light.

And it seemed to hover above the tracks – not quite touching them.

Joe peered round the side. The train wasn't long – just a single compartment with a single door. There was no sign of a driver.

Smoothly, silently, the door slid back, revealing a bright orange interior.

"Woof!" Pippy wagged her tail.

"Look, Joe." Scarlett peered inside. "There are two big chairs and a TV screen and –" she craned her neck further round the door – "someone's left some clothes on a table too…"

With a bark, Pippy jumped on board.

For a second, Scarlett hesitated, then she leaped after the dog.

"Pippy, Scarlett, come back!" Joe yelled. Honestly, that was so typical of Scarlett – rushing into things without checking them out first. Joe crept closer to the door, taking in the big orange chairs. What kind of train had only two seats?

A blank TV screen ran down one side of the compartment. Beyond it, at the end of the carriage, Scarlett was standing beside the table, holding up a white pinafore. Pippy padded over to her.

"Pippy, come here," Joe said, firmly.

Pippy stared at him with her big brown eyes. "Woof!" She wagged her tail.

Joe sensed she was trying to reassure him. Scarlett had put down the white pinafore and was now holding up a pair of long, dark-brown shorts.

"Wow," she said, her eyes shining. "They're

17

like dressing-up clothes, Joe. Girls' stuff *and* boys'."

Joe took a deep breath and climbed into the train compartment. He grabbed Pippy's collar and looked round. "This is well weird," he said.

"I know." Scarlett was now examining a blue dress. "Look at this, it's really heavy – but isn't the colour *beautiful*?"

Joe shook his head. He picked up a coarse white shirt from the table. It was a boy's shirt. About his size and similar to the one he wore for school – though made of much rougher and heavier material. Orange writing on the inside of the collar caught his eye.

Scarlett held the dress out in front of her.

"I'm going to try it on," she said, all excited.

Joe rolled his eyes. Trust Scarlett to treat this bizarre experience as an excuse for playing dressing up.

"It's not yours," he pointed out.

But Scarlett already had the dress half over her head.

Joe frowned, then looked back at the orange writing on the inside of the shirt collar. *No.* He peered more closely. It couldn't be...

Joe Simmons. The orange words spelled out his name.

3 TAKEN!

Joe stared at the embroidered writing on the shirt, unable to believe his eyes.

"Look at this," he gasped.

But Scarlett wasn't listening. "Look at *me*." She twirled round in the blue dress. The long skirt floated out around her legs.

She picked up the white pinafore again and held it up in front of her. Four white straps hung

from the central white panel. "I reckon this goes over the dress," she said. "How d'you think it ties up, Joe?"

Joe stared at the pinafore. A glimpse of orange on one of the straps caught his eye. He snatched the pinafore out of Scarlett's hands.

"Hey," she complained. "I was just…"

"Look." Joe held out one of the straps. The name *Scarlett Simmons* was written in orange along the edge. "It's like it's for you." He showed Scarlett the shirt collar with his name on it. "And this one's for me."

Scarlett stared at the words, then looked up at him, her eyes wide. "But who put them here?" she said.

"I don't know."

At that moment the TV that ran along the side of the compartment burst into life with a series of colourful pictures.

21

Scarlett's mouth fell open. "What the…?"

Joe stared as a street full of narrow, brick houses filled the screen. A thick white stripe was painted along the road. A line of children in old-fashioned clothes, like the ones Joe and Scarlett had just found, were walking along the street.

Joe blinked. "This is *really* odd." He looked around. "What's making the TV work?"

There were no knobs or switches beside the screen – there was nothing that they might have touched by accident, and no remote control or computerized handset either.

"Joe!"

He turned back. Half the screen was now filled with a large block of clear, white writing.

"Read it, Joe."

Joe read out loud:

MAY 1941. THE BLITZ, LONDON.

Alfie Suggs, aged 10, died a hero's death yesterday when a bomb exploded in his house at 4.05 p.m. Alfie left the safety of an air-raid shelter to warn his deaf grandmother that the sirens were sounding.

"He was such a good boy. Always putting others before himself," Mrs. Suggs said. "He knew I wouldn't hear the siren, so he ran to warn me. I'd got out of the house before the bomb fell, but Alfie was trapped inside. I'm his nan and I will miss him for the rest of my days."

"That's so sad." Scarlett's face was pale.

"Yeah," Joe agreed. "Poor Alfie…"

Joe's phone beeped. A text.

"That's probably Mum, wondering where we are," Scarlett said.

Joe pulled the mobile out of his pocket. But

instead of the usual sign saying, *New message*, the phone had somehow gone into stopwatch function. It was counting down from an hour – fifty-nine minutes and fifty-nine seconds...fifty-eight seconds...fifty-seven...

The hairs on the back of Joe's neck stood on end. What on earth was happening?

Scarlett peered over his shoulder. "Why's your phone—?"

Slam! The train door slid shut.

"What's going on?" Scarlett cried.

The train filled with that strange, thin *whee* noise it had made before. And then everything happened at once. The compartment jolted. The engine throbbed. And the TV screen vanished, leaving a clear glass window in its place.

Outside, the grass was speeding past.

"We're moving!" Joe shouted. "The train is taking us away."

4 THE BOY

The train went faster and faster. Joe gripped one of the orange chairs and stared through the window. They were moving so speedily now that everything outside was a blur.

"Where are we going?" Scarlett shrieked.

"I don't know." Joe's heart hammered in his chest. None of this made sense. Questions sped like bullets through his brain. Where had this train come from? Where was it taking them? How were they going to get home?

Pippy barked. She was still wagging her tail, as if everything that was happening was just a great big adventure. A minute or two passed and then, gradually, the blur outside the window sorted itself into shapes.

"I think we're stopping," Joe said.

He peered through the window as the train drew to a standstill. They were underground, looking out over a station platform. It was dark – just a few candles and lanterns casting a spooky glow across the walls.

The platform was crowded with people in coats and hats. Some of them huddled together against the walls. Others were making little camps for themselves, with cushions to sit on and bags and baskets of food and papers. No one was looking at Joe and Scarlett – or the train.

"What's going on?" Scarlett said. "Why are all these people here?"

"I don't know." Joe's heart beat even faster than before. He'd seen a picture of people in old-style clothes crowded onto an underground station before, at school. But his head was spinning so much that he couldn't remember what they'd been doing down there.

"Look, Joe." Scarlett's voice was breathless. "Look at what you're wearing."

Joe looked down. His own clothes were gone. He was dressed in the brown shorts and white shirt they'd found earlier.

He glanced at Scarlett. The white pinafore was now neatly tied round her waist, over the blue dress she'd put on herself.

"How did that happen?" he said.

Scarlett shook her head. She pointed outside. "We're dressed like they are," she said.

Joe looked through the window again. It was true. There were several children on the platform – some scampering about, others sitting with their families. Most of the boys were dressed in long shorts, while the girls all had on heavy, rough dresses similar to the one Scarlett was wearing.

"This is *really* weird." Scarlett's voice was low and shocked.

"I know." A shiver snaked its way down Joe's back. And then a thought struck him. Why was no one looking at the train? It was right next to the platform that everyone had crowded onto, yet none of the people out there was looking either at the train – or at them – through the window.

"They can't see the train." Joe said, the truth slowly dawning. "It's like it's invisible or something."

"Woof." Pippy nuzzled Joe's legs, then trotted over to the train door.

"Maybe we should get out and ask someone for help," Scarlett suggested.

"The train might just start moving again," Joe said. "Maybe *we* can make it move." He looked around for any sign of driving equipment, but there was nothing...no machinery...no levers... no switches...

Scarlett bit her lip.

Over by the train door, Pippy barked.

"Looks like Pippy wants us to go outside," Joe said.

Scarlett nodded. "Well at least then we could find out where we are." She went over to Pippy and stood beside the train door. "How does this open?"

As Joe walked over, the door slid magically back.

"Come on, then," he said. And the three of them stepped onto the platform.

The first thing that struck Joe was the noise – a wailing siren that filled the air. The second was the terrible smell – a sour, damp combination of stale sweat and musty clothes and a couple of other things Joe really didn't want to think about.

A woman sitting against the wall, feeding her baby, glanced up at them.

"He'll never sleep with all this noise," she sighed. She bent over the baby again.

"They can see us now," Scarlett whispered.

Joe nodded – the train might be invisible but, clearly, he, Scarlett and Pippy weren't once they were outside it. The three of them made their way down the platform. There was something very familiar about the scene around them, but Joe still couldn't work out what. He felt completely bewildered by everything that had happened – and that siren noise was piercing through his head.

Scarlett tugged at his sleeve. "Who shall we ask?" she said.

Joe looked round. Mum always said that if they got lost they should find a woman with children and ask her for help. But all the women nearby were in groups, chatting with each other. Joe, Scarlett and Pippy walked on. They passed two men playing cards and a clutch of girls in a corner, who stared at Scarlett's wild, red hair.

"Nice dog," said a freckle-faced boy in long brown shorts and a grubby shirt. He grinned, making a crease across the muddy smear that marked his cheek, then patted Pippy's back. "Is she yours?"

"Yes," Joe said. "Er...where are we?"

"We're at the station, pal," the boy said.

"Didn't you notice which shelter you went into when the air-raid warning started?"

Shelter? Air raid?

"But what town are we in?" Scarlett said.

The boy raised his eyebrows. "London, of course."

Joe and Scarlett exchanged glances. How on earth had the strange train brought them to *London*. They'd only been travelling a few minutes.

"Well, nice to meet you," the boy said. "But I gotta go before the air raid starts."

Of course. Joe's breath caught in his throat. *London. Air raids.* That wailing noise in the background was an air-raid siren. They used them in wars to warn people that bombs might be dropped out of planes. To tell them to go to air-raid shelters. Joe's heart skipped a beat.

He was sure there hadn't been a war where

London got bombed by planes since…

"Bye then," the boy said.

"Wait. What time…I mean, *when* is it?" Joe said.

"*What*, pal?" The boy wrinkled his nose. "'Ere, you two are a right pair. Can't help you, though. I ain't got no watch."

"I don't mean the time of day." Joe gulped. "I mean…what *year* is it?"

The boy laughed. "The year Britain's gonna win the war, pal."

"What war?" Scarlett turned to Joe. "What's he talking about?"

But Joe's eyes were fixed on the boy.

"What do you mean, 'what war'?" The boy took a step away. "Look, I've really got to go…"

Joe grabbed his arm. "Wait, please. I know it sounds crazy, but we need to know which war and which year it is."

"All right, pal, take it easy. It's 1941 and we're fighting the Germans." The boy spoke slowly and clearly, as if Joe and Scarlett were idiots. "Cheerio." He turned and walked away.

Joe's heart pounded as everything fell into place. So *that's* why the train had shown them the old film. It was showing them where it was taking them.

"I don't understand," Scarlett whispered.

"We've gone back in time," Joe said, slowly. "Back to the Second World War."

5 THE WARNING

Joe stood still, letting the truth sink in. It didn't feel real. Surely, it *couldn't* be real. With a jolt he realized why the scene in the station seemed familiar. He'd seen pictures of places just like this in books and on the internet when they'd done a history project on the Second World War at school.

The train juddered into life behind them.

It made its strange, thin *whee* sound.

"Joe, look!" Scarlett shrieked. "It's leaving!"

"No!" Joe shouted. But it was too late. Before he could move, the train glided silently away and was out of sight.

"Where's it going?" Scarlett gripped his arm. "What's happening? How can we be in the Second World War? That was years and years ago."

Joe shook his head. He felt completely bewildered.

The boy they'd been talking to had reached the steps leading up to the station exit. Joe dashed towards him, trying not to trip over the people sitting on the platform. He caught up with the boy as he clambered over the sandbags someone had laid against the bottom step.

"Stop." He grabbed the boy's arm as Scarlett ran up beside them. "Wait."

"I told you, I'm in a hurry." The boy shook Joe's arm off. "I gotta find my nan before the air raid starts. She went deaf a few months ago. Doesn't hear the sirens."

Joe stared at him. Find his *nan*? But that was what the boy they'd heard about in the train had been doing…and during an air raid, as well.

He glanced at Scarlett. She was frowning.

"What's your name?" Joe said.

"Alfie," the boy said. "Alfie Suggs."

It was the same boy.

Joe and Scarlett exchanged looks.

"No way." Scarlett shook her head. "This is mad."

The boy rolled his eyes. "If you ask me, it's you two that's blinking mad." He raced away up the stairs.

The air-raid siren was still wailing all around them. Joe's stomach churned.

"Come on," he said and ran after the boy.

He, Scarlett and Pippy followed Alfie up the stairs, along a short corridor and then up a stationary escalator.

As they reached the top, fresh crowds of people surged towards them. Just a few metres ahead, Alfie was struggling to get past everyone too.

"Alfie," Joe shouted. "Stop."

Alfie glanced over his shoulder. "Get lost."

"*Joe.*" Scarlett panted up beside him. "What are you doing?"

"That's the same boy from the TV on the train," Joe said, making way for a large woman with a fluffy cat in her arms. "We have to warn him about the bomb that's going to go off."

"But…"

Joe didn't wait to hear what Scarlett was

saying. He pressed on, finally reaching Alfie as he hurried up to the station exit.

"You mustn't go home," Joe said, as Scarlett arrived. "You…you'll be hurt."

Alfie frowned. "What?"

"Please listen, Alfie," Joe said desperately. "You need to stay here, where it's safe."

"Who d'you think you are, pal?" Alfie's frown deepened. "You're soft in the head if you think I'm gonna let you tell me what to do."

"You have to listen," Joe went on, feeling desperate. "It's not safe at your home. If you go back there a bomb's going to fall and… and…"

Alfie raised his eyes. "And you know this because you can see into the future, I suppose?" he said.

"Not exactly." Joe bit his lip. This was impossible.

"Actually, we're *from* the future," Scarlett explained.

Alfie stared at them. "You *are* mad." He shook his head. "No, wait. *Now* I get it," he said. "Jack Stephens put you up to this, didn't he? Well, you can tell him I ain't falling for it." He raced off.

"Come on," Joe said. "We have to follow him."

"Wait," Scarlett said, her face screwed up with concern. "I want to help Alfie too, but don't you think we ought to be trying to find the train so we can get back home?"

"Helping Alfie *is* our way of getting back home." The words were out of Joe's mouth before he knew he was going to say them. But, straight away, he was sure they were true. "I don't understand why or how, but it wasn't an accident that those clothes were waiting for us on the train. Or the story about Alfie and his nan. We're *supposed* to be here."

"What are you talking about?" Scarlett said.

Alfie had now disappeared out of the station. Joe grabbed Scarlett's arm and strode after him.

"Let me go," she said.

Joe held her arm more tightly. "Don't you see?" he said. "The train brought us here for a reason. I'm sure it did. It showed us the story about Alfie being killed by the bomb, like...like it was giving us a mission."

"A mission?" Scarlett stopped trying to pull away. "A mission to save Alfie from being killed?"

Joe nodded. Beside him, Pippy barked.

"Wow." Scarlett hesitated for a second, then her mouth set in a determined line. "Well, come on then."

6 THE MISSION

Outside the siren was still wailing and the sun shone fiercely. Joe shielded his eyes from the glare and looked round.

This was weird.

The street in front of him was more or less deserted – just a few stragglers still making their way towards the station. It looked the same as the street they'd seen on the TV screen in the train, even down to the thick white line painted along the road. What was that for?

Alfie was turning the corner up ahead.

"Come on," Joe said. He and Scarlett raced down the street, Pippy scampering at their heels. Joe gazed round as he ran.

At least the houses were normal enough – brick buildings with small front gardens. Then he saw the house on the corner. It looked like it had been peeled open with a tin opener. The front wall was stripped away, leaving the insides on show. On the first floor a fireplace still stood in the corner of the room. A battered picture hung above the mantelpiece.

"Did a bomb do that?" Scarlett panted as she ran, her red curls damp against her forehead.

Joe nodded, grimly. The air-raid siren was still screeching all around them. Joe realized he'd been so preoccupied with warning Alfie not to go home, that he'd forgotten that the siren was warning everyone about the bombs.

He'd learned about it at school. This was the Blitz, a time during the Second World War when lots of bombs were dropped on London. Other cities were attacked too, as part of the enemy's plan to defeat Britain.

They turned the corner after Alfie. He was quite a way down the road, running hard.

"Alfie, stop," Joe yelled.

As Alfie glanced over his shoulder, he tripped over a rusting, red metal tricycle. It lay on its side, as if its owner had been hauled off it in a hurry.

Alfie stumbled to a halt, rubbing his shin. At that moment the siren stopped.

"Stop following me and get back to the station before the bombs start," Alfie shouted. "Lunatics like you shouldn't be wandering the streets."

"We're not lunatics." Joe caught him up. "Scarlett was telling you the truth. We've come from the future and…"

"On what?" Alfie's eyes widened. "A ruddy flying carpet?"

"No…" Joe hesitated as Scarlett joined him. "Some kind of train…"

Alfie snorted.

Pippy barked as a round-faced man in a tin hat emerged from the junction ahead.

"What's going on here then?" The speaker raised his thick eyebrows and frowned at Alfie. "Why aren't you down the shelter, Alfie – and where's your gas mask? Your nan'll have your guts for garters if she knows you've been out without it again."

"Sorry, Mr. Parks," Alfie said. Now the siren had stopped Joe was aware of how silent it was with no people or cars about. "Just gotta make sure my nan heard the siren," Alfie went on.

Mr. Parks took off his tin hat. The letters ARP were painted across the front. "Your nan'll be fine, Alfie. Mrs. Jones is keeping an eye on her. What *you* need to do is take your mates and hop it back to the shelter."

Alfie made a face.

"*Now*, son," Mr. Parks said.

"Yes, Mr. Parks." Alfie turned and trudged back down the street.

Joe and Scarlett grinned at each other. "Thank goodness for that," Joe whispered.

"And you two an' all," Mr. Parks went on.

"Yes, sir," Joe said. He and Scarlett caught Alfie up at the end of the road.

Mr. Parks was still watching them, making sure they left. They turned the corner, but had only gone a few paces, when Alfie ducked down an alleyway and sped up again.

"What are you doing?" Joe said.

"This isn't the way back to the shelter," Scarlett added.

"You don't think I'm doing what I'm told, do ya?" Alfie grinned. "This is the long way home... so we avoid bumping into that warden again... old Parksy."

And before Joe could say anything, he was off again.

Alfie ran fast, down several streets. Joe and Scarlett kept up with him, Pippy running alongside.

At last Alfie stopped – in the most bomb-damaged street they'd seen so far. Half the road was destroyed. It was full of rubble, like a giant digger had just scooped up a huge handful of houses and thrown them back down on the ground. A row of sandbags, like the ones by the stairs at the station, were heaped in a pile across the road from the few houses that were still standing.

A dull thud sounded in the far distance.

"What was that?" Scarlett said.

Alfie turned round. "That was a bomb." He shook his head. "It isn't a game, this war, you know."

A low hum drifted faintly across the air. Joe guessed it was coming from one of those old-fashioned planes. Loud *ack-ack* noises followed.

"What's that?" Joe asked.

"Guns," Alfie said. He opened a rusty gate and raced down the front path towards the house beyond. It was small and narrow like its neighbours – part of a section of the street that was still standing. However, it was the only house Joe could see that wasn't boarded up at the windows.

"Guns?" Joe said, following Alfie down the path.

"Shooting from the planes?" Scarlett glanced round. "Where?"

Alfie rolled his eyes. "No, you lunatics, they're *our* guns. They're trying to shoot down the Jerries' planes."

"Jerry's planes?" Scarlett frowned. "Who's Jerry?"

"Jerries are Germans," Alfie sighed. "Don't you know *that*?"

Joe squinted at the sky. He could just make out a couple of black dots in the distance, zooming past a line of fluffy clouds.

"How far away d'you reckon those planes are?" he asked.

"A few miles," Alfie said, fumbling for a key in his pocket. "I've got to hurry."

Joe took a deep breath. Pippy nuzzled round

his legs and he bent down and stroked the dog's back.

"Then we'll come in with you," he said, "and help you find your nan."

7 ALFIE'S HOUSE

Alfie was clearly too worried about his nan to argue with them.

"You look for her downstairs," he said. "I'll check the bedrooms – she's deaf, remember, so she won't hear you shouting."

As he opened the door a dog howled nearby.

Pippy barked a reply.

"Is that your dog?" Scarlett asked.

Alfie shook his head. "Nah. That's Big Rex. He's mad…lives a few doors up. His family got bombed out…everyone killed except him."

They walked inside. The hallway was short and narrow – just one door on the left, and one at the end of the corridor.

As Alfie ran up the stairs, Joe opened the door on the left and peered inside. It was empty, apart from an open fireplace and two high-backed armchairs. All very neat and tidy. The clock on the mantelpiece said 3.35 p.m.

Joe suddenly remembered that the TV on the train had told them the bomb that killed Alfie exploded at 4.05 p.m.

He pointed out the time to Scarlett. "At least that means we've got half an hour to get out of here," he said.

The floorboards creaked upstairs as Alfie ran across the landing. He was muttering to himself.

A series of faint thuds sounded in the distance.

"Those bombs sound further away than the ones we heard before," Scarlett said.

"Yeah." Joe relaxed slightly. It was okay. The bomb wasn't coming for thirty minutes. They had time.

They heard Alfie thunder down the stairs and went back to the hallway. They followed him through the door at the end of the hall into a small kitchen area with a spotless black-and-white tiled floor. A stack of enamel bowls stood by the big sink. Above the sink was a window and next to the window, the back door. Joe peered through the window onto a narrow back garden containing a strip of grass and a vegetable patch beyond.

"Where *is* she?" Alfie muttered.

The room tracked round in an L shape to a larger, messier space.

Joe took the other part of the room in quickly. A row of black-and-white photos had been squashed along the mantelpiece above the fireplace. A wooden table laid with a tablecloth was set against the far wall. A rubber mask lay on the table. It had protruding plastic eyes and a long rubbery tube coming out of the front.

"Ugh." Scarlett made a face. "What's that?"

"My gas mask. You're supposed to take them with you everywhere." Alfie stared around the room, as if he were hoping his nan would suddenly materialize in front of them.

Outside, another round of faint thuds sounded in the far distance.

"We were wondering…" Joe paused. "Those bombs, they sound like they're getting further away?"

"Yeah, over the docks, maybe." Alfie nodded. "Just wish I knew where Nan was. Maybe she

went to the shops." He sighed. "It's just she usually has a nap about this time, so…"

"Do you live here with your nan?" Joe asked.

"Yeah, most of the houses on the street are boarded up. The council says the whole road's unsafe. But Nan won't leave. Says she won't let the Jerries turn her out of her home."

"What about your mum and dad?" Scarlett asked.

There was a pause. More distant explosions sounded outside. Big Rex, the mad dog from down the road, howled again.

"My mum died ages ago," Alfie said, staring at the table. "My dad's in France."

"What's he doing there?" Scarlett asked. Joe prodded her. There was a war on. What did Scarlett think Alfie's dad would be doing?

Alfie looked up. "Fighting the Jerries, of course."

Another pause. Joe didn't know what to say. He couldn't imagine what it must be like to have no mum and your dad away, fighting in a war.

Joe pushed the thought away. The planes might be further off now, but he was sure they would be back. If Alfie's nan wasn't here then there was no point in them hanging about.

A plane droned overhead. Alfie looked up, nervously.

"Sounds like a Heinkel 111," he said.

"We should go," Joe said. "I—"

WHAM! An earsplitting boom filled the room. Everything shook – like an earthquake was ripping the house apart. The force of it threw Joe off his feet and onto the floor. He lay, face up, winded. The room erupted into dust and rubble around him.

Everything moved in slow motion. Plaster fell softly off the walls. Plates from a dresser he hadn't noticed before spun through the air. A white jug twisted slowly above his head. Joe opened his mouth to scream.

CRASH! The jug smashed onto the floor by his ear.

Time sped up again.

"Aaargh!" He could hear himself screaming. A weird, high-pitched sound that didn't seem to come from his own mouth. He was dimly aware of other screams around him.

Then silence. He struggled to his elbows, coughing. The room was dark, filled with thick dust. He could see nothing. His eyes stung. It was hard to breathe through the choking dust.

Panic filled his whole body.

"Scarlett!" he yelled. "Alfie! Pippy!"

The silence was as thick as the dust now settling on his head and shoulders. Joe scrambled to his feet, fear clawing at his throat.

"Scarlett!" he yelled again. "Pippy!"

He held his breath, waiting for a reply. But the only sound he could hear was the rapid *duh-dud*, *duh-dud*, of his own heartbeat.

8 TRAPPED

For one terrible moment Joe thought he was going to cry. Then he felt the solid slap of Pippy's tail against his legs. He reached down and a warm, wet nose pushed itself into his hands.

"Pippy."

The dog snuffled at his palm. Joe patted her back and blinked the dust out of his eyes. It

was still dark in the room, but his eyes were becoming accustomed to the gloom.

"Joe?" A figure covered in grey dust emerged from behind the table, which now lay on its side.

"Scarlett? Are you okay?"

"I think so." Scarlett looked around the room, her eyes wide and dazed. Pippy trotted over and nuzzled her legs. Scarlett stroked the dog's head. "Where's Alfie?"

"I'm here." Alfie hauled himself up from the other side of the wooden table. He was covered in the same grey dust as the others.

"You two look like ghosts," Joe said.

"So do you, pal," Alfie said as he looked round the room.

"What happened?" Scarlett asked.

"Must've been a bomb next door. Reckon we caught the shockwave off it." Alfie turned to Joe,

his face pale under the grimy smears. "I hope my nan wasn't out there."

Joe bit his lip.

"I've got to find her. Make sure she's all right." Alfie picked his way across to the kitchen area. "Blimey, this is a mess," he muttered.

Joe followed him, thinking the devastation around them was quite a bit more than *a mess*. But he didn't say anything. Alfie looked anxious enough. The kitchen was unrecognizable. The whole back wall – including the back door and window – had disappeared from view, hidden by rubble. There was a large hole in the high ceiling way above their heads.

Joe stared up at it – the shockwave from next door must have been massive to have caused this much damage.

And why would it create a hole in the ceiling? He frowned.

"Hey, Joe," Alfie said, sounding like he was trying not to cry. "Help me with this."

He was yanking on the door that led into the hallway. It didn't open. Joe went over and pulled at the door too. It stayed firmly shut.

"Must have got stuck when the bomb fell," Alfie said. "Maybe we can move some of this rubble and get out the back way." He started pulling at some of the smaller bits of brick and plaster that blocked the back door and window.

"Joe," Scarlett whispered. "That story in the train was wrong. A bomb *has* fallen, but Alfie hasn't been killed. He's safe. We're all safe. We just have to get out of here."

"Sure." Joe nodded, but he didn't feel safe. They were still stuck inside a bombed-out building – and there was something about that hole in the ceiling that didn't make sense.

At that moment the siren started again but, this time, instead of the two repeated wails it sounded a long, single note.

"What's that?" Scarlett asked.

Alfie shook his head. "Don't you two know anything?" He pulled angrily at a large, rough bit of rubble blocking the back door. "That's the all-clear. It means the raid's over. We're safe for now."

At least that was one less thing to worry about. But Joe still didn't like the forceful way Alfie was wrenching at the rubble heaped against the back door. A small avalanche of bricks cascaded down the pile. Alfie jumped back.

"Maybe that's not such a good idea," Joe said. They might be safe from more bombs falling, but the house was still, clearly, a dangerous place to be.

Alfie ignored him. He bent down and carried

on pulling at bricks. The walls creaked. More rubble fell.

"Stop, Alfie," Joe said. "You'll bring the whole ceiling down on top of us."

Alfie turned on him, frustration etched on his face. "Well, how're we going to get out, then?" he shouted. "The door to the hall is stuck and the back door and window are blocked off with all these stones and stuff. So, come on, pal, if you're so clever, tell me how we're going to get out of here?"

9 THE BOMB

Joe and Alfie stared at each other.

"Alfie?" A muffled voice called from the back garden. "Alfie, is that you?"

Alfie leaped up. "Mrs. Jones?" he yelled. He turned to Joe and Scarlett. "She's our neighbour – her house backs on to this one."

"Are you all right, duck?" Mrs. Jones shouted.

"Fine," Alfie shouted back. "Is Nan with you? I came back to warn her about the siren, but she isn't here."

"Your nan's right as rain, duck, or she will be when you get out of the house," Mrs. Jones yelled.

Alfie grinned at Joe and Scarlett, relief written all over his face.

"I nipped over earlier to bring her down to my shelter," Mrs. Jones went on. "She was spitting nails about you not taking your gas mask to school. Now listen, you need to get out of there, fast."

"I can't," Alfie shouted. "The front door's stuck."

"Oh goodness. I'll fetch the warden." Mrs. Jones's voice suddenly grew urgent. "I'll be back in two shakes."

"Okey dokey."

"Er...sit tight, Alfie," Mrs. Jones went on. "Don't get yourself upset. Er...can you see it?"

Joe frowned. *What was she talking about?*

"See *what*?" Alfie sounded confused too.

"Nothing," said Mrs. Jones. "Er...keep your chin up. Back soon."

Joe wandered across the room, still puzzling over what Mrs. Jones had said. All the black-and-white photos that had lined the mantelpiece now littered the floor. One small, grainy picture of a family group caught his eye. He picked it up.

"That's me when I was a nipper, with Mum and Dad and Nan and Grandad." Alfie peered over Joe's shoulder. "Guess we're going to have to move out now like they want us to. Nan's going to hate it. She's lived here all her life. Says this house has all her memories."

Joe didn't know what to say. He offered Alfie the photo.

Alfie pointed to his trouser pockets. "They're torn," he said. "Would you keep it for me till we get out of here?"

"Sure." Joe stowed the picture in his own trousers. It clinked against his mobile. He took the phone out. It was still stuck in the stopwatch function for some reason – *twenty-one minutes and three seconds…two seconds…one…*

What was going to happen in twenty-one minutes?

Joe sighed. Yet another mystery on a day full of them.

"S'pose we just have to wait for Mrs. Jones to get back with the warden," Alfie said. "He'll bring someone to dig us out. There's a Warden Station about fifteen minutes away but it's always chaos after a bomb raid. It'll be ages till they're back."

Joe let out a long breath. There was nothing

they could do now except wait. At least the air raid was over.

"Joe," Scarlett sounded worried. "Come here."

Joe picked his way across the room to where Scarlett stood in front of the pile of rubble that blocked the back door. Pippy was sniffing at the bricks.

"What?" Joe said.

"Look." Scarlett pointed to a small hole in the rubble near the bottom of the pile.

Joe squinted into the hole. At first he couldn't see anything, it was too dark.

"D'you see it?"

"What?" Joe strained his eyes. After a few more seconds they adjusted to the blackness.

Joe could just make out a length of curved black metal. His heart skipped a beat as he turned back to the others. They were watching him intently.

"What is it?" Alfie said.

Joe looked up at the hole in the ceiling above their heads. He could see clear through to the white clouds above. Whatever was underneath the rubble had obviously fallen from the sky, through the house.

The truth hit Joe like someone had picked up a piece of brick and whacked him round the head with it.

No wonder there was a hole in the ceiling. *That* was why Mrs. Jones had wanted them to hurry out of the house. *That* explained why she'd asked if they could *see it*.

Joe took a deep breath. "That bomb we thought fell somewhere really near," he said. "It's here. It just didn't go off."

"*What?*" Scarlett's eyes widened. "You mean that story on the train was right, after all?"

"What are you talking about?" Alfie

70

demanded. He pushed his way in front of Joe and stared through the tiny hole in the rubble. He stood silently for a moment, staring at the bomb, then turned back.

"Must be from that Heinkel I heard," he muttered.

"Why hasn't it exploded?" Scarlett said.

"Sometimes they don't straight away." Alfie caught Joe's eye. "Which means it could go off any second."

"*No*," Scarlett gasped.

Joe nodded. This *was* the bomb the train had told them about. He tried to think back to the story they'd been shown. Alfie had gone to warn his nan, but his nan was already outside the house and Alfie was trapped inside... *Yes.* That was exactly what had really happened. He racked his brains, trying to remember if the story had told them anything else. No, only that the

bomb was going to explode at 4.05 p.m. The clock in the front room had said the time was 3.35 p.m. That had been about ten minutes ago, which meant it must now be about 3.45. That only gave them twenty minutes before the bomb went off.

A thought suddenly struck him. He pulled his mobile out of his pocket. The countdown was still in progress...*twenty minutes and twenty-nine seconds...twenty-eight seconds... twenty-seven...*

Everything slid into place. Joe could hardly believe it, but it was the only explanation that made sense.

"I think the countdown on my mobile is linked to the bomb going off," he said hesitantly.

"Your mobile what?" Alfie said.

Joe shoved the phone in front of Alfie's nose so he could see the numbers counting down.

"It started counting down just after we found out about you and the bomb," he said.

Alfie's eyes widened as he stared at Joe's phone. "Where did you get that?" he said suspiciously.

Scarlett turned to Joe. "It started as soon as we found out about Alfie on the train, didn't it?"

"Yes." Joe stared at the numbers ticking by on the screen. His stomach twisted over and over.

"So what's going to happen when the countdown gets to zero?" Scarlett asked, uncertainly.

Joe took a deep breath. "The bomb explodes." He glanced at the stopwatch again. "Which means we've got precisely nineteen minutes and fifty-five seconds to find a way out of here."

10 THE ONLY WAY OUT

Joe, Scarlett and Alfie stared at the pile of rubble hiding the unexploded bomb.

"I don't know why you're so flipping sure that bomb's going to go off in nineteen minutes," Alfie said, his voice tight with anxiety, "but there's no way Mrs. Jones and the warden'll be back here by then *and* get us dug out."

Joe's heart thudded. "We have to find a way

out ourselves, then," he said.

"How?" Alfie made a face. "All the ways out are blocked…"

"What about climbing up through there?" Scarlett pointed to the hole in the ceiling above their heads.

Joe and Alfie looked up. The hole was two metres or so above the top of the pile of rubble.

"It's too high up," Alfie said. "We wouldn't be able to reach it."

"And anyway, we'd have to climb up all that to get to it." Joe pointed to the pile of rubble that covered the bomb. "We don't want to bring down any more, it might set the bomb off."

His mouth was dry. He turned round and stared at the only other way out of the room – the door into the hallway.

"Let's try this again," he said. "I mean, the door itself isn't damaged, it's just got all jarred against the frame because of the bomb. Maybe we can shift it if all three of us try."

They lined up together and gripped the handle.

"One, two, three," Joe counted.

They pulled as hard as they could. The door didn't budge.

"Great idea, Joe," Scarlet said, grumpily.

Irritation mingled with the fear in Joe's guts. "Well you suggest something then if you're so clever."

Scarlett tossed back her hair, creating a light cloud of dust around her head, like a halo. She stared carefully around the whole room. Her eyes fixed on the dust-covered kitchen floor, where Pippy, her dark fur covered in grime, was sniffing at a piece of fallen brick.

"Maybe we can dig our way out," she said.

"With what?" Joe rolled his eyes. "Teaspoons?"

"No. Wait." Alfie slapped his forehead, as if just remembering something. "We don't have to dig. There's a cellar under the kitchen."

"Where?" Joe looked around. The kitchen was covered in rubble and dust. A row of cupboards on one wall led into the pile of masonry containing the bomb. Everything else was hidden from view.

Alfie pointed to the row of cupboards, at a door that looked slightly bigger than the others. "The cellar's through there, but the top steps are broken. We don't go down there any more, it's dangerous."

He fell to his knees and began pulling away the bricks that blocked the base of the door.

Scarlett and Joe exchanged glances.

"Don't we need to get *away* from the house?" Joe said.

"You don't understand." Alfie ran his hand

through his hair. The dust made it all stand up on end so that he looked like some kind of mad professor. "All the cellars in the street are connected by these little doors. They used to be almshouses, charity houses for poor people. If we can get through to the next house…"

"…we can get away from the bomb." Joe grinned, hope flickering at last.

He kneeled down and helped Alfie shift a particularly big piece of masonry from the floor. As soon as it was free, Alfie leaped up and pulled open the cellar door. Joe peered into the dark space below.

"That's it," Alfie breathed.

It was pitch black…and impossible to see how far down the floor was. All Joe could see was that, as Alfie had said, the top steps were broken. There was nothing solid to put your feet on to.

"We'll have to jump," Alfie said.

Joe realized his hands were shaking and clasped them together so the others wouldn't see.

"How much time, Joe?" Scarlett asked.

Joe checked the countdown. "Seventeen minutes and forty seconds."

"That should be enough time to get out, shouldn't it?" Scarlett asked.

"If we can get through to next door," Alfie said.

"I'll go first." Joe swung his legs over the edge. He hesitated a second. He didn't like heights – he'd been frightened of them ever since some bully had pushed him off the climbing frame when he was in the infants'. Still, this was no time to be a baby. And at least not being able to see the floor meant he couldn't see how far he had to fall. Pippy trotted over and licked his hand. That made him feel better.

"It's been ages since I went in there, but I don't think it's too far down," Alfie said.

"Only one way to find out." Joe eased himself down so that his legs were now dangling between the broken steps.

He looked up, into Alfie's and Scarlett's anxious, dust-smeared faces.

"Here goes," he said. And he jumped into the gloom.

11 THROUGH THE DARK

Joe landed with a thud. The cellar floor was only half a metre below his dangling legs, and slightly squelchy underfoot. He laughed with relief that he was down safely, not minding the musty smell of damp.

"Have you got any candles, Alfie?" he yelled. "It's really dark down here."

Footsteps. A minute later Alfie's oval face

appeared above Joe's head. He jumped down, took a couple of candles out of his pocket and lit them. Scarlett coaxed Pippy over to the broken cellar steps and helped her through to Joe.

As Scarlett followed Pippy, Joe buried his face in the dog's rough fur, just for a second, breathing in her warm, reassuring smell. Then he set her down.

Alfie handed Joe a candle. "Don't waste it," he muttered. "Candles don't grow on trees, you know. Nan had to give up our butter ration to get the last lot."

Nodding, Joe took a candle. The light only properly illuminated a small patch of dusty floor and Scarlett and Alfie's faces, ghost-white, beside him.

Joe peered into the shadows. Cobwebs hung everywhere – great, thick sheets of them.

"Wow," Scarlett said, her eyes wide and

shining in the candlelight. "Lucky I'm not afraid of spiders."

"There should be two doors, at opposite ends of the cellar. They'll take us to the houses on either side of this one." Alfie peered at a dark shape propped against the nearest wall. "Look, that's my old push-along horse. I thought Nan had thrown it away."

Joe wandered away from the others. "D'you remember where the doors are?" he said.

Alfie's voice echoed out of the gloom. "Not exactly... I'll look over here."

Joe held his candle against the bare brick wall. He'd reached the corner of the room. They just had to do this systematically, examining the walls bit by bit. Right here was almost empty – just some old paint tins propped in front of the wall. He moved along, Pippy sniffing at everything beside him. He passed some bits of damp wood and what looked like part of an old chair – all covered in thick wreathes of cobweb.

And then he saw it – a small wooden door bolted against the brick wall; a padlock fastened to the handle.

"Hey I've found a door," Alfie shouted from across the room.

"I've found the other one," Joe yelled back.

"Well, how about opening them?" Scarlett said. "Seeing as we could blow up any second."

Joe checked his phone. It showed that the bomb was going to explode in sixteen minutes and seventeen seconds. "We should still have enough time," he said, "provided we can get through here okay."

"That countdown thing of yours...?" Alfie said. "How does...I mean where did you get it?"

"We told you," Scarlett said. "The future."

Alfie shrugged. Even in the dim candlelight across the room it was clear he didn't believe them.

Scarlett nudged Joe. "Imagine what he'd say if he knew you could make phone calls on it."

Across the room, Alfie fumbled with his bolt.

"There's a padlock," he shouted. "I can't see a key."

Joe stared at his own door. There was no key for the padlock on that either. All the energy seemed to drain out of him as he looked at the door. Maybe the bolt would slide back, but the padlock was too much to deal with. It was rusty, like all the other metal things down here, but there was no way Joe could unpick it.

No way out.

"What's going on?" Scarlett demanded.

Joe pointed at the padlock. "There's no key." As he said the words, a terrible sob rose up in his chest. His nose prickled and two fat tears bubbled into his eyes.

Pippy barked. Joe was sure she was trying to reassure him, but it was no use. They were going to die.

"Wait a minute." Scarlett reached out, pulled back the bolt, then yanked at the padlock. It came away in her hand, along with the rusty brass plate that attached it to the door. She turned to Joe, beaming. "Everything down here's like a million years old. It's all falling apart."

Joe stared at his sister. "You're a genius," he said.

Pippy barked again.

Scarlett shrugged. "Whatever." She pushed at the door. It creaked slowly open, revealing the deep darkness of next door's cellar.

"Come on, Alfie," she called. "We're through."

They found the stairs up to next door's kitchen

straight away. Joe just had time to worry that Alfie's neighbours might have bolted their cellar door from the kitchen side, when he was at the top of the stairs, side by side with Alfie, pushing it open.

12 OVER AND OUT

The room they emerged into was a kitchen similar in shape and size to Alfie's, but much dirtier and emptier. Joe glanced at the stained sink in the corner and the cupboard doors hanging awkwardly off their hinges. He tried the back door, while Alfie raced through to the front.

"Front door's locked," Alfie shouted. "And the windows are all boarded up."

Joe rattled the back door handle. "This one's locked too," he yelled.

"But look." Scarlett picked up a long key lying beside the sink. She held it out to Joe, triumphantly.

Joe's hands shook as he turned the key in the lock and opened the door. Debris from Alfie's house next door had fallen into the back garden, though the fence between the two houses was still standing firm. The sun was shining out here and the air was much clearer than it was inside the houses. Joe breathed in lungfuls of fresh air, while Pippy bounded down the garden.

Alfie raced after her. "Come on," he called. "We can get out through the garden gate. There's an alley behind. We just have to move this roller."

Joe looked up. Alfie had reached the tall wooden fence that ran across the bottom of the garden. A large rusted roller machine stood propped against the gate that led out to the alley.

Alfie yanked at the roller. "Help me," he called, "it's really heavy."

Joe and Scarlett ran over. The roller was huge and made of metal. Its cylinder was broken – one end was partly missing, leaving a jagged edge that made the whole roller slump slightly sideways against the earth.

The cylinder was stained white.

"What's that for?" Scarlett asked, pointing at the white paint.

"For making those white marks on roads. To show people the way to the shelters in the blackout."

Joe remembered the white line on the road that they'd followed earlier.

The three of them grabbed the roller handle

and pulled. The roller wobbled a bit, but didn't move away from the gate.

Joe checked his phone. The countdown showed thirteen minutes and six seconds before the bomb went off.

"How much time?" Scarlett asked.

"Enough," Joe said.

They tried again, but although the roller teetered for a second, it didn't move away from the gate.

Joe stopped, panting for breath. "What's it doing here, anyway?" he said.

"The man who used to live here collected scrap metal – old bits and pieces. Sold them for cash," Alfie explained. "Maybe no one's realized this broken roller is still here. If we can't shift it away from the gate, we can just get on top of it and climb over the fence." He leaped up onto the cylinder.

It teetered slightly on its jagged edge.

"Alfie…" Joe began.

With a yelp, Alfie lost his balance and fell to the ground. He landed heavily, his right leg twisted underneath him.

"Aargh!" he cried. "Aargh, my ankle!"

Joe dropped to his knees. "Are you okay?"

"No." Alfie's face was grey. "It hurts."

Now how were they going to get out? The fences at the bottom and sides of the garden were high. He and Scarlett could just about climb them, but could Alfie manage? Joe checked his phone again. Twelve minutes and ten seconds to go.

"Come on." He grabbed Alfie's arm. "We have to get out of here. Can you stand up? Can you put any weight on that ankle?"

Alfie swayed as Joe hauled him to his feet. He put his foot gently to the ground, then winced.

"No," Alfie said, a look of panic in his eyes. "I can't walk, let alone climb."

"But we have to get out of the garden." Scarlett caught Joe's eye.

"Not without Alfie," Joe said, firmly.

Pippy barked.

"I'll just *have* to, then." Alfie took a step forward, then collapsed again, his face twisted with pain.

"I know." Joe pointed to the roller. "We're going to have to shift that away from the garden door." He went over and pushed at the roller again. But, as before, it was too heavy for him to lift.

He sank onto the ground, defeated.

"What are we going to do?" Scarlett's voice rose in panic.

Joe swallowed. After all they'd been through, he couldn't believe it.

"You don't have to stay," Alfie said, his voice trembling.

"Yes we do," Joe insisted.

He looked at Scarlett. She nodded.

"We're going to get you out of here before that bomb goes off," Joe said.

"How?" Alfie asked.

"We'll work it out," Joe said.

But the truth was, he had no idea.

13 HELP!

Pippy bounded up, tail wagging. Joe barely noticed her. How on earth was he going to move that huge roller so they could get Alfie out through the garden gate?

"What are we going to do?" Scarlett said. "There's hardly any time left..."

Joe checked his phone again. She was right. Just under eleven minutes until the bomb went off.

"When d'you think the warden will get here, Alfie?" he said.

"Could be ages, yet."

"I'll go and find someone else."

"There's not enough time." Alfie's voice shook. "Hardly anyone lives in the street any more. By the time you've found someone and got back, it'll be too late."

Joe stared at the roller. Maybe if he found something to act as a lever, he could prise the roller away from the door. He picked up a branch from the ground and placed one end under the metal cylinder. But as he pressed down on the other end, the wood snapped in two.

"What are you *doing*, Joe?" Scarlett's voice rose.

Joe stood back, his stomach churning. Pippy nuzzled at his hand. "I think I might be able to lever the roller up, but I need something stronger to do it with," he said.

He followed Scarlett's gaze round the garden. There were one or two bits of scrap metal left in the garden – but nothing large enough to be of any use.

Come on, Joe, think.

He stroked Pippy's rough, wiry fur. "Hey, girl," he said. "Can you find anything we could use?"

Pippy looked up at him with her bright brown eyes, her head cocked to one side. Then she bounded off, sniffing round the garden. Joe peered behind bushes and shrubs.

Nothing.

He wasted a couple of minutes opening the door of what looked like a tool shed next to the house, but it was just an outside toilet.

He checked his phone again as he ran back to Alfie and Scarlett. Eight minutes and forty-one seconds to go.

"I'm going to climb over the fence into next door's garden," he said. "See if there's anything we can use there."

"Hurry up," Scarlett yelled.

"Watch out for Big Rex," Alfie shouted.

But Joe barely heard them. He was looking round the garden for Pippy. Where was she? He stared at the place in the fence where he'd last noticed her. Several planks of wood at that spot were broken. He looked more closely. There was a tiny hole at the bottom of the fence which she must have squeezed under. He couldn't follow her though. The hole was too small for Scarlett to fit through, let alone Joe.

"Pippy!" he called.

But she didn't come running and Joe knew he didn't have time to go looking for her. Reluctantly, he turned towards the fence leading to the garden on the other side. It was lower than the one Pippy had snuck under, easier for him to climb.

With a grunt, he hauled himself over, into the garden next door. It was empty – overgrown and full of weeds. There was nothing here he could use as a lever.

The fence to the next garden was really high. If it wasn't for a sawn-off tree trunk halfway along there was no way Joe could have got over it. He clambered onto the trunk, then reached up, breathing heavily, as he climbed onto the fence.

Joe paused at the top for a second to catch his breath. A sick feeling swelled in his stomach as he looked down. There was no sign of Pippy, but the next garden was full of junk that might be useful. Feeling rather dizzy, he leaped into it.

An open tin of congealed varnish lay on its

side; a box of nails, the contents scattered across the scrubby grass, stood beside it.

Joe stepped over these, his pulse racing. *There.* A long, curved metal pole, with a raised, flat end, like a spade, was propped against the house wall.

Joe had no idea what it was for, but it was the perfect shape and length for levering that metal roller away from the door.

He checked his phone – six minutes and thirty-five seconds until the blast. He picked up the metal pole. It was only as he turned that he realized there was no tree trunk on *this* side of the high fence – which meant there was no way for him to climb back over. His heart slumped into his shoes. How was he going to get back to Alfie and Scarlett now?

"Woof." The bark was deeper and fiercer than Pippy's.

Joe spun round. A mangy dog – lean and wiry, with bald patches in its fur – stood, growling, in front of him. One ear was torn so that the tip hung ragged, at an angle.

Joe's heart leaped into his throat. Was this the dog they'd heard howling earlier? The one Alfie said was mad?

"Nice doggy," he croaked. "Good boy."

The dog bared his teeth and padded closer.

Joe backed away. What had Alfie said the dog's name was? Roy? Rover?

"Rex?" he said. "Big Rex?"

The dog barked, as if acknowledging the name, then resumed his low snarl. Saliva dripped from his mouth as he advanced on Joe.

Joe took another step backwards, then another. He was almost backed up against the house now.

"Come on, Big Rex," he said. "No reason to hurt me."

Who was he kidding? Big Rex didn't look like he needed a reason!

Bump. Joe came up against the brick wall of the house. He turned his head slowly. The nearest window into the house was an arm's length away – and boarded up. The fence Joe had just climbed over was several metres away. He had to get back there.

He waved the long metal pole at the dog. Big Rex bared his fangs and howled. Joe flattened himself against the wall.

In the distance he could hear Scarlett yelling out his name, but he couldn't call back. He could barely breathe.

Big Rex looked evil. Like he hadn't eaten for a week and Joe was lunch.

14 BIG REX

Big Rex pawed the ground like he was ready to pounce. He howled again. Joe pressed his body harder against the wall behind him. The bricks were rough and cold on his back and under his sweating palms. Beside him a rusty metal drainpipe reached up to the roof of the house. Maybe he could climb the drainpipe – get away from Rex that way? He glanced up.

The drainpipe led to a sloping roof. Joe's head spun at the sight of it. It was too high...too far off the ground.

He turned back to Big Rex, still snarling just in front of him.

"Help!" he yelled as loudly as he could. "HELP!"

A few seconds passed – they seemed like hours – and then an answering bark came from a distant garden.

Joe recognized it immediately.

Big Rex turned his head.

"PIPPY!" Joe yelled. "Over here."

As soon as the words were out of his mouth, he wished them back. Big Rex was twice Pippy's size. She'd stand no chance in a fight. But seconds later she was wriggling under a broken plank in the fence and through the bushes. She raced up to Joe, barking.

Big Rex turned. He growled – a low, menacing rumble.

Joe's chest tightened. "No, Pippy," he shouted. "Go away. *Please.*"

Pippy barked, backing away from Big Rex. The mangy dog followed her, turning his attention at last from Joe.

This was Joe's chance to get away.

He chucked the metal pole over the fence into next door's garden, then he grabbed the rusty drainpipe beside him.

It was the only way. If he climbed up onto the first-floor roof, he could crawl along that, past the high fence, then leap down into next-door's garden, grab the metal pole and get back to the others.

Maybe if he moved fast, he wouldn't notice how high up he was.

Joe took a final glance at Pippy. She was still

barking her head off. Big Rex was growling back, his teeth bared and ready to attack.

Pippy turned and fled beneath the bushes. Big Rex dived after her.

This was it.

Joe hurled himself at the drainpipe and hauled himself upwards. The rust was rough on his hands. Praying the thing would hold his weight, he climbed hand over hand, like a monkey, pressing his feet against the wall on either side of the pipe. Seconds later he reached the roof.

He grabbed hold of the gutter above his head, pushed away from the wall and swung himself up. One elbow over. Then the other arm. Then his knee. Yes, he was there. He pulled himself up into a crouch and glanced down.

Big mistake. He was at least three metres off the ground. A new panic surged into his throat.

106

His breath quickened and the ground below seemed to spin.

He turned away and tried to focus on what he had to do next. Crawl across the roof to next door, then lower himself into the empty garden to pick up the metal pole he'd thrown over the fence earlier. He didn't want to waste time – and risk losing his balance – taking his phone out of his pocket, but he knew there had to be less than five minutes until the bomb exploded.

Joe's heart raced. Gritting his teeth, he edged along the roof. He kept his gaze on the tiles under his hands and knees, partly so as not to slip and partly so his head didn't spin from seeing how far off the ground he was.

He crawled across to the next house. Now he *had* to look down. The ground was terrifyingly far away. As Joe stared, the grass

beneath seemed to sway, like a weed-ridden sea. His stomach responded with its own sickening lurch.

Focus.

There was the metal pole. No sign of Big Rex or Pippy. Joe looked across to the next garden. There was Alfie, sitting on the ground clutching his ankle. Even from this distance, Joe could see how pale his face was. Scarlett, sitting beside him, looked up. Straight away, she caught sight of Joe.

"Hurry," she called.

Joe nodded. He shot a quick glance along the alley that ran behind the houses. There was no sign of Alfie's nan or the warden or anyone hurrying down the passageway that led to the end of the gardens.

It was all up to Joe.

"I'm almost there," he yelled.

Bump! His foot slipped from under him. He fell, outstretched, onto the roof. He slid down, unable to get a grip on the tiles ripping past his fingers.

Falling.

15 THE SCOOP

Joe clattered over the tiles – knees, chin, elbows bumping furiously against the roof. He clawed for a hold, his fingers and palms scraping against the tiles.

His legs slid over the edge of the roof. Their weight pulled the rest of him down. His body was over. Slipping. Now his chest. Sliding down. His arms outstretched. With a final, massive effort he grabbed the gutter with his fingers.

His arms felt like they were being wrenched out of his shoulders as his fall finally ended. Joe hung by his hands for a second, catching his breath, then he looked down. He was hanging over the empty garden. The ground swam beneath him. Joe's heart raced. His head spun.

Just let go, he told himself. It's not that far to the ground. *Just let go.*

He clung on, his fingers rigid, his arms aching from carrying his weight.

You're being stupid. Stupid.

It was no good. He was too scared to move. Too scared to do anything. He closed his eyes, trying to stop the whirling inside his head.

The moment his fear of heights had started – when he'd fallen off that climbing frame and broken his arm – flashed into his mind. The same panic filled him.

111

And then, in the distance, he heard Pippy's reassuring bark.

Joe's eyes snapped open. He had to jump. He had to save the others. He had to complete the mission.

Joe let go of the gutter. The ground rushed up to meet him. *Wham.* He landed lightly in an overgrown flower bed. *Yes.* He'd done it!

But there was no time to congratulate himself. He spun round and headed for the metal pole. As he picked it up he checked the time.

Two minutes and twenty-nine seconds.

He hurled the pole over the fence into Alfie's garden, then pulled himself up by his exhausted arms. Every muscle in his body ached. But he couldn't stop now.

"I'm back," he yelled, dropping down into the garden.

"About time." Scarlett sounded cross – but Joe could hear the fear underneath her anger.

"What did you find?" That was Alfie.

"A metal pole, like a curved mop handle."

"A mop handle?" Alfie sounded incredulous.

For the first time Joe wondered if his plan was going to work.

"How much time before…?"

"Loads," Joe lied. He slid half the metal pole under the roller that blocked the door.

"You found a scoop." Alfie sounded impressed. "They're for raking up firebombs."

"Yeah?" Joe pressed down on the other end of the pole. The metal shifted slightly. With a bit more weight behind it, this might just work. "Scarlett come and help me."

Scarlett raced over. She put her hands next to Joe's, gripping the pole tightly.

"I'm going to count to three," Joe said. "On

three, we push down just enough for the roller to move away from the door."

"Okay," Scarlett said.

Joe took out his phone and gave the screen a swift glance. One minute exactly. Sixty seconds...fifty-nine...fifty-eight...

This *had* to work.

"One." He shoved the mobile in his pocket.

"Two." He gripped the pole with both hands and braced his feet against the earth.

"Three." Joe pressed down as hard as he could. Next to him, Scarlett grunted as she pressed down too. Every aching muscle in Joe's body tensed with the effort.

Yes. With a groan the roller shifted and slid away from the door. Joe and Scarlett dropped the pole.

"Come on," Scarlett yelled.

Between them, they helped Alfie to his feet.

Scarlett fumbled with the bolt on the garden door, pulling it back, while Joe let Alfie lean on his arm, as he limped across the grass.

Scarlett opened the door. A few seconds later, they were all through and into the alleyway. Free.

"How much time?" Scarlett asked.

Joe checked his phone one last time. "Twenty seconds."

"What?" Scarlett yelped.

Joe hooked his arm under Alfie's shoulder. "Run," he yelled. "RUN!"

16 EXPLOSION

Joe counted down the seconds in his head.

Eighteen… Seventeen…

They pelted down the alley, Joe half holding, half dragging Alfie beside him.

Sixteen… Fifteen…

Round the corner, into the street. An old lady and the man in the tin hat who'd stopped them earlier were up ahead.

Fourteen… Thirteen…

"STOP!" Alfie yelled at them. "It's Nan and Old Parksy," he said to Joe and Scarlett. "They're going to the house. STOP!"

Twelve… Eleven…

Nan and Mr. Parks stopped in their tracks. Mr. Parks looked up, confused.

"BOMB!" Alfie yelled. "BOMB! NOW!"

Ten… Nine…

No time to explain. Joe pointed to the pile of sandbags on the other side of the road. "OVER THERE!" he yelled.

Eight… Seven…

Mr. Parks put his arm round Nan and hustled her across the street.

Six… Five…

Joe grabbed Scarlett's hand, still supporting Alfie on his other side. He dragged them both towards the sandbags.

Four... Three...

Nan was looking round at Alfie. Mr. Parks yanked her behind the sandbags.

Two...

Alfie, Joe and Scarlett dived after them. Alfie winced as he hit the ground.

One.

WHAM! The explosion vibrated through the air. The ground shook. Joe ducked down behind the sandbags, covering his head with his hands. He could feel Mr. Parks's arm across his back. Scarlett huddled next to him.

Rubble and metal fell all around them. Joe's eyes were tight shut but he could smell the burning and feel a thick layer of dust falling on his shoulders. Alfie's nan coughed. And then, at last, there was silence.

The arm lifted off Joe's back.

"You all right, son?" Mr. Parks said.

Joe looked up. The man's round, reddish face was full of concern.

"Yeah." Joe stretched out his arms and legs. Relief washed over him like a wave. They'd done it. They'd escaped from the bomb. He glanced at Scarlett, then over the sandbags at Alfie's house. His mouth fell open. It had gone. A crater full of bricks and rubble stretching into both the next-door houses stood in its place. Small fires were dotted across the wasteland.

Joe shivered at how close they had come to being part of the blast.

"You okay, too, miss?" asked Mr. Parks.

Scarlett nodded. She smiled at Joe. "Mission accomplished," she whispered.

"Alfie!" Alfie's nan pulled him into a hug. "Oh, Alfie, are you all right?"

Her voice was thick as she spoke, but her words were clear.

"I'm fine, Nan." Alfie pulled away, so she could see his mouth. He spoke slowly and clearly. "I hurt my ankle, but I'm okay. No need to fuss."

Nan looked over Alfie's dust-covered head. "You two Alfie's chums? I don't think I've seen you before."

"They saved my life, Nan," Alfie said.

Nan beamed at Joe and Scarlett. Then she looked over the sandbags, towards the house. Her face crumpled. She turned away, so they couldn't see her expression.

Joe shuffled awkwardly. He looked again at where Nan had been staring; at the remains of her and Alfie's home.

Scarlett put her hand on Nan's arm. "I'm sorry about your house."

Alfie repeated what she'd said more slowly, emphasizing each word.

Nan nodded, blinking back tears. "All our memories." She sighed. "I suppose we would have had to leave some time, but not like this." She shook her head and put her arm round Alfie again. "There's nothing left. That's what gets me, duck. Nothing. A whole life, lots of lives, all gone."

"Least your boy's safe," Mr. Parks said gruffly.

Alfie translated.

Nan nodded. "I know."

She squeezed Alfie again. He looked over at Joe and Scarlett, clearly pleased but a bit embarrassed.

Nan smiled. "My Alfie being safe's the most important thing."

Scarlett nudged Joe. She pointed at his trouser pocket.

"Oh." Joe remembered the photo of Alfie's

family that he'd said he'd look after. He took it out of his pocket and handed it to Nan.

"Er...Alfie thought...er...you'd want this. I found it after the bomb dropped...kept it for you."

Nan took the photo and stared at it. Her eyes filled with tears as she looked up at Joe. "Thanks, duck," she said. "You have no idea what this means to me."

"So what happened?" Mr. Parks asked.

As Alfie started explaining, Joe stood up. A small crowd had gathered nearby. He could hear people muttering about the bomb.

"Was anyone hurt?"

"No, but some nippers only just made it out."

"Hope it got that mad dog down the road. Blooming terror, he is."

Joe froze. *Dog.* Never mind Big Rex. Where was Pippy?

"Pippy?" he shouted. "Pippy?" He waited a second, sure she would bark, or appear, racing down the road in response to his call.

But she didn't.

Scarlett clutched at his sleeve. "Joe, where is she?"

Joe cupped his hands to his mouth, to make his shout louder.

"Pippy?" he yelled again, frantic now. "Pippy? Where are you?"

17 FINDING PIPPY

"We've got to find Pippy," Scarlett said. "Where did you last see her?"

Joe thought for a moment. The last time he'd actually *seen* Pippy had been when she was distracting Big Rex away from him. But he'd *heard* her after that – barking when he was dangling from that gutter. She'd sounded close then.

He looked over to the half-destroyed houses on either side of Alfie's home. There was no way a dog – or anything, for that matter – in or near those houses could have survived the blast.

Surely Pippy had got away?

"Joe?" Scarlett tugged at his sleeve.

"I saw her in one of those gardens when I was looking for something to help get you and Alfie out," Joe said, remembering how brave Pippy had been. "She distracted the mad dog from down the street who was attacking me."

Scarlett breathed a sigh of relief. "She must have run off then. She can't have gone far."

Joe shook his head. He wasn't so sure. Suppose Big Rex had chased her for miles. She might be lost. Or hurt.

"You talking about your dog, pal?" Alfie frowned. "Where is she?"

"Around somewhere," Scarlett said.

"I'm going to look for her," Joe said.

"Hold your horses," Mr. Parks said. "You and your sister need to come down the ARP Station with me. Your parents will be worried sick about you."

Joe and Scarlett exchanged glances.

"Our parents aren't from here," Scarlett said quickly.

Mr. Parks frowned. "What d'you mean?"

"We're...we're..." Joe struggled to remember the word. "We've been evacuated."

Mr. Parks stared at him, blankly. Joe's throat tightened. Had he got the word wrong? He was sure that during the Blitz loads of kids were taken from their families and sent away from home.

"Evacuated *into* London?" Mr. Parks frowned. "I don't think so. Maybe you're being sent out to the country, to where it's safer?"

"No." Joe looked round, desperately. They had to get away, find Pippy...get back home.

Home.

Joe suddenly remembered the way the train had zoomed out of the underground station and disappeared. That had only been an hour ago, but it felt like days. Mum had texted them to come home for their tea just before the train had shown up. She must be worried sick.

How on earth were they going to get back?

"We just need to find our dog," Scarlett said firmly. "Then we'll go straight home. Promise."

Joe edged away from the others. He had to find Pippy. Right now, that was all that mattered.

Alfie limped over, leaning on Scarlett's shoulder. "Wait up, pal," he said.

"You should go back to your nan," Joe said.

"Wait." Alfie grabbed his arm.

Joe stopped. "What?"

"I'm sorry I didn't listen to you earlier, about the bomb, I mean." Alfie glanced over his shoulder to make sure Mr. Parks wasn't listening. "I...that is, are you...I mean, you knew a bomb was going to go off...I'm sorry I didn't believe you."

Joe nodded. "It's fine. But right now I *have* to find my dog."

"So...so are you *really* from the future?" Alfie went on.

"Course we are," Scarlett said.

Alfie frowned. He looked very serious. "Then would you mind telling me something?"

In the small part of Joe's mind that wasn't focused on Pippy, he could see that whatever Alfie wanted to know was very important to him.

"Sure," he said. "At least, I'll do my best."

Alfie took a deep breath. "This war. The war

against the Jerries. Er…who wins?"

Joe grinned. Even he knew that one. "We do," he said.

Alfie grinned back. "I knew it. I'm going to tell Nan."

"She won't believe you any more than you believed us," Joe said.

Alfie shrugged.

"Where will you live now?" Scarlett asked.

"My auntie's up north, I expect," Alfie said. "She's asked us often enough."

Joe smiled and turned to Scarlett. "We've got to find Pippy. Now."

"Where d'you think she is?" Scarlett looked worried.

Joe shook his head. "Dunno, but we've got to get away and look for her." He glanced over at Mr. Parks. He was still busy talking with Alfie's nan.

"Bye Alfie," Joe said. Weird to think that only this morning he hadn't known Alfie even existed. "Good luck."

"You too," Alfie smiled. "I hope you find your dog."

Scarlett leaned over and kissed his cheek.

Alfie pinked. "Cheerio."

Joe and Scarlett darted off down the street, dodging the lumps of brick and metal scattered across the ground.

"Oy!" Mr. Parks yelled. "Come back."

Joe rounded the corner. Nothing was going to stop him finding Pippy. Nothing and no one. She had to be here.

He slowed slightly as he reached the next street, taking enough time to make sure Pippy wasn't sheltering in any of the front gardens he was passing.

"Let's try down here." Joe darted towards the

alley that ran down the back of the houses in Alfie's road. He peered down it. No sign of Pippy.

He and Scarlett raced on, round corners and down more and more streets. They ran past a line of shops – a butcher's with a queue of people outside and a grocer's with *Business as usual* written in chalk on its boarded-up window.

Still no sign of Pippy.

At last, worn out, Joe stopped. He leaned, panting, against a lamp post. They were just outside a park. A woman with a huge pram on outsize wheels wandered past.

In the distance a dog barked.

Joe turned round. Another bark. Was that Pippy? The sound was so faint he couldn't even be sure which direction it was coming from.

"Did you hear that?" Scarlett jumped up and down.

"Yeah. D'you think it was Pippy?"

Scarlett stopped jumping and stared at him. "What d'you mean? I heard that weird *whee* noise the train makes."

Before Joe could say anything the ground beneath them rumbled and the sky darkened.

"Look!" Scarlett shouted. "It's coming!"

18 HOME

The train sped towards them across the park. Invisible to everyone except Joe and Scarlett, it hovered, as before, over glowing, magical tracks – past trees, round the children's play area, and over a duck pond. Seconds later it whooshed through the park gates and drew to a halt on the pavement, right beside Joe and Scarlett. It stood, its glow fading, as the sky brightened again.

"Yay!" Scarlett cried. "It's come to take us home."

"What about Pippy?" Joe said.

The train door swished open. Scarlett jumped on board. "Pippy'll be here," she said. "The train won't leave her behind."

"Pippy!" Joe's heart hammered against his throat as he followed Scarlett into the train. "PIPPY!"

The engine gave a throb.

"No!" Joe leaped off the train. He stared wildly round at Scarlett, still standing inside the carriage. "No, it can't go yet."

"It's not *going* to go," Scarlett insisted.

The train's high, thin *whee* screeched through the air. Its single compartment juddered and rocked.

Scarlett's eyes widened. "Okay, it is. Get back on board."

"PIPPY!" Joe strained his eyes into every corner of the park. His stomach twisted over and over. Where *was* she?

"Joe, please! It's moving!"

The train glided across the pavement. Scarlett reached through the open doorway and grabbed Joe's arm.

"Let go," Joe yelled. "I'm not going without Pippy."

Scarlett held on to his arm.

"Pippy!"

The train moved faster. Joe had to run to keep up with it. Scarlett gripped his arm tighter.

"PIPPY!"

Yes. There she was, galloping towards them round the corner, Big Rex racing after her.

Joe held out his arm. Pippy leaped up. Joe clutched her to his chest. He jumped into the train. Big Rex bounded up.

The train door closed in Big Rex's face as Joe and Pippy landed in a heap – Joe hugging Pippy. Pippy scrabbling over his face. Scarlett, underneath them both, yelling furiously.

A moment later, the train whooshed smoothly away.

Joe rolled over. Scarlett wriggled away. For a second they both sat, silent, stroking Pippy's rough, wiry fur.

Joe looked up. As before, everything through the window was a blur. Then the window magically vanished, to be replaced by the TV that ran down the side of the carriage. The screen filled with moving pictures.

"Hey, look." Joe smiled. "There's Alfie and his nan."

The film showed a busy railway station. Nan and Alfie were bustling along the platform. Pushing their way onto a crowded train.

Seconds later the scene changed to show them getting off the same train in a country station surrounded by green hills. A young woman greeted them both with a hug.

"That must be Alfie's auntie," Scarlett said, a satisfied expression on her face. "That means they're okay."

Joe nodded. The screen went blank, then filled with words.

"Hey, Scar, listen to this." Joe read out loud:

Alfie Suggs, aged 10, proved yesterday that not all our heroes are overseas. Young Suggs left the safety of his air-raid shelter to warn his deaf grandmother that the sirens were sounding. A high-explosive bomb fell into the house, trapping the boy – but did not explode on impact. Suggs and two unnamed friends escaped unharmed before the bomb went off.

"Alfie's such a good boy. Always putting others before himself," said Mrs Suggs, Alfie's grandmother. "I'm lucky to have him…"

Scarlett beamed. The train roared to a stop. The TV screen went blank immediately. Pippy barked.

"I think we're supposed to get off now," Joe said.

"No kidding." Scarlett stood in front of the carriage door. "I want a bath with some of Mum's designer bath foam."

"But you're not dirty any more." Joe stared at her, then at himself. They were as clean as when they'd boarded the train earlier. In fact, Joe realized with a jolt, they were back in their original clothes. When had that happened?

Scarlett looked down at her jeans. "Oh,"

she said, sounding disappointed. "I liked that dress."

"Whatever." Joe followed her, Pippy at his heels. Honestly, sometimes Scarlett didn't have much of a grip on what was really important. Who cared about a dress?

As they stepped out of the train, they found themselves back in the park where they'd been playing ball over an hour before. Instantly the train and its tracks vanished, leaving no trace they had ever existed.

Joe shook his head. There was still so much about what had happened they didn't understand.

"Why d'you think the Time Train picked *us* to help Alfie?" Scarlett said.

"Dunno," Joe said. "But that's a good name for it…Time Train."

As they left the park and walked home,

Joe's thoughts shifted to Mum. Was she going to be cross they'd been away for so long? But, as they let themselves in through the back door, she was bustling about in the kitchen.

"Hiya," she said. "Tea's on the table."

"Good." Scarlett sat down at the table. "I'm starving."

Joe shook his head. Mum had texted them over an hour ago, saying tea was ready *then*. It was as if they hadn't gone back in time at all. Or as if going back in time hadn't taken any time out of the present.

As he went next door to the living room, he could hear Scarlett telling Mum about the Time Train and their journey to the Blitz. From Mum's *Really?* and *Ah, I see*, he could tell Mum didn't believe a word of it.

Joe stared out at the back garden. Pippy snuffled into his hand.

For a minute he wondered if he'd imagined the whole mission.

And then a faint *whee* sound echoed across the trees.

A few moments later, Scarlett rushed in. "Did you hear that?"

Joe nodded.

"Mum didn't." Scarlett shook her head in disbelief. "I told her what happened but I think she thought I was making it up – like it was some imaginary game."

"Yeah." Joe grinned. "But we know it was real, don't we?"

They stood in silence for a few minutes, waiting. But the Time Train didn't sound again.

"D'you think we'll ever…you know…go on another mission?" Scarlett said.

Pippy barked.

"I hope so," Joe said.

141

Scarlett sighed. "Me too."

And, with Pippy beside them, they went into the kitchen to have their tea.

THE END